Furry Friends

Look out for these other
special short story collections by

Enid Blyton

Magic and Mayhem
The Great Outdoors

Enid Blyton

Furry Friends

Illustrated by Mark Beech

HODDER

HODDER CHILDREN'S BOOKS

Content previously published in Great Britain in *Animal Stories* (2019),
Nature Stories (2020) and *Pet Stories* (2021) by Hodder & Stoughton
This edition published in 2022

1 3 5 7 9 10 8 6 4 2

Enid Blyton® and Enid Blyton's signature are
registered trade marks of Hodder & Stoughton Limited
Text © 2022 Hodder & Stoughton Limited
Illustrations © 2022 Hodder & Stoughton Limited

A CIP catalogue record for this book is available from the British Library.

ISBN 978 1 444 94680 2

Printed and bound in Great Britain by Clays Ltd, Elcograf S.p.A.

The paper and board used in this book are made from wood from
responsible sources.

Hodder Children's Books
An imprint of Hachette Children's Group
Part of Hodder & Stoughton
Carmelite House
50 Victoria Embankment
London EC4Y 0DZ

An Hachette UK Company
www.hachette.co.uk
www.hachettechildrens.co.uk

Contents

The Kitten That Disappeared

The Kitten That Disappeared

JOHN AND ROSIE had a kitten of their own. It was three months old, as black as coal, with eyes as green as a cucumber. It was the merriest, lovingest, warmest little kitten you can imagine, and the two children loved it with all their hearts.

It was called Fluffy, and it always came when it heard its name. It was very mischievous, and loved to hide under the beds or under the chairs and pounce out at people's toes. Fluffy loved everyone and everyone loved Fluffy.

And then one day she disappeared. It was the most extraordinary thing. One minute she was playing with the two children in the kitchen and the next minute she was gone!

Mother was busy. It was Monday morning and she had a lot to do. She had washed up. She had done the laundry and put the dirty sheets and towels into the big basket for the laundry man to collect. She had made the beds and peeled some potatoes for dinner. And all the time Fluffy had played about with the children, sometimes jumping up at Mother, sometimes trying to catch her apron strings as she whisked here and there.

Then she was gone!

'Mother, where is Fluffy?' said Rosie, looking around.

'Hiding somewhere, I expect,' said Mother, fastening up the laundry basket in a hurry because she heard the laundry man coming down the passage.

'Fluffy, Fluffy!' called John – and there came an answering mew from somewhere, very tiny. 'MiiaOOOW!'

'She's somewhere!' said John, and the children began to look under the dresser and under the stove. The laundry man rang the bell, and Mother gave him the laundry basket. She shut the door so that Fluffy shouldn't run out if she were hiding somewhere. John called again. 'Fluffy! Fluffy!'

But no matter how he listened he couldn't hear another mew. No, Fluffy didn't answer at all. Rosie hunted under the bottom shelf of the broom cupboard, and then in the cupboard where the newspapers were kept. But Fluffy wasn't anywhere to be found!

'Oh, Mother, Fluffy has quite, quite disappeared!' said Rosie, almost crying.

'Don't be silly, darling,' said Mother. 'She must be somewhere about. She is hiding. Perhaps she has slipped upstairs and gone under one of the beds.'

'But, Mother, the kitchen door has been shut all the time,' said John. 'She simply must be in the kitchen if she is anywhere.'

'Well, she'll turn up all right,' said Mother. 'Don't

worry. I haven't time to help you hunt now, but when I've finished making this pudding for your dinner I will have a look around. But I expect by that time that Fluffy will come dancing out from somewhere!'

But, do you know, she didn't! So when Mother had finished making the pudding and popped it into the oven to cook, she had a look around for Fluffy too. She put down the saucer of milk and fish for the kitten, and called her.

'Fluffy, Fluffy, Fluffy! Puss, puss, puss! Dinner, dinner, dinner!'

But still no Fluffy came dancing out on black velvety paws! Rosie cried big tears.

'Mother, it's magic! Some fairy has taken Fluffy away!'

'Nonsense, darling!' said Mother, laughing. 'The fairies never do unkind things. Fluffy may be in the garden.'

So they put on their coats and hunted all around the garden. No Fluffy. They went to the house next door, but Mrs Brown hadn't seen their kitten at all. They went to Mrs White's too – but she hadn't seen Fluffy since the day before.

Well, the children hunted and called all morning, but Fluffy was not found. They had their dinner, and then hunted again.

'Never mind,' said Mother. 'Fluffy will come in when she is hungry.'

'Mother, I don't think she ever went out,' said John. 'I don't really. One minute she was playing hide-and-seek with us, and the kitchen door was shut, I know – and the next minute she had disappeared.'

Although Mother put a saucer of fish and milk in the garden as well as in the kitchen, no Fluffy came to eat it – and Mother began to get worried too. She was very fond of the little black kitten and she could *not* think where it had got to. But at last she knew!

There came a ring at the kitchen door. Mother went to open it – and there was the laundry man, grinning all over his red cheerful face. In his hand he held a box.

'Good afternoon, Mrs Jones,' he said. 'I just wanted to tell you that you had sent this to the laundry, but as it seems quite clean we wondered if you really *did* want it washed!'

He opened up the little box he carried – and in it, curled up, was Fluffy! How the children shouted and danced for joy! Mother stared at Fluffy in astonishment.

'Whatever do you mean?' she asked the man.

'Well, madam, when we opened your laundry basket at the laundry, we found this little black kitten fast asleep inside!'

'Good gracious!' said Mother. 'She must have jumped inside when she was playing hide-and-seek with the children – and I didn't notice her – and shut down the lid! Then you took the basket away with Fluffy inside! We did hear a faint mew from somewhere – she must have been in the basket then!'

How glad Fluffy was to see the children again! How she pranced and danced on her four paddy-paws!

How she licked up her fish and milk! How she mewed and purred! What a fuss was made of her!

'Oh, Mother! Fancy sending our kitten to the laundry!' said Rosie. 'Suppose she had been washed and ironed, whatever would she have thought!'

It's a good thing the laundry *didn't* wash and iron Fluffy, isn't it? She *did* have a narrow escape!

Good Dog, Rover!

Good Dog, Rover!

ROVER BELONGED to Robin and Mary. Sometimes he could be very good but at other times he could be very naughty. It didn't seem to matter which he was, though; the children loved him just the same.

One day Robin gave Rover a juicy bone to gnaw. 'It's good for your teeth,' he said. 'And you've been such a good dog lately I think you really do deserve a bone!'

'Miaow!' said Tabby the cat. She liked bones too, though she could only scrape them with her rough tongue – she couldn't manage to chew them.

Rover looked at her, with the bone in his mouth.

He dropped it for a moment and spoke to her.

'You can miaow all day if you like,' he said. 'But you won't get so much as one single sniff at this bone.'

'Wherever you bury it I shall find it,' said Tabby. She was very clever at finding where Rover buried his bones, and he didn't like it. It was too bad to bury a half-chewed bone, and then, when next he came to dig it up, to find that it wasn't there because Tabby had found it.

'I shan't bury it this time,' said Rover. 'I shall hide it where you will never be able to find it!'

He trotted off with the bone. He took it into the dark tool shed, and lay down to chew it. It was a very hard bone and Rover couldn't crunch it up. He had a lovely half-hour of chewing and gnawing. Then he heard Robin whistling for him.

'Walkie, walkie, Rover!' called Robin, and Rover knew he must put away his bone and go. But where should he put it? It must be somewhere clever, where Tabby would never find it. Rover thought of all the garden beds in turn. No, Tabby would hunt in each one. Then he looked around the tool shed. Tabby never came in here! He would hide his bone somewhere in the tool shed.

He was lying on a sack. What about tucking it inside the sack? Then no one would see, and it would wait here for him to come back and chew it. That would be a fine hiding place.

So Rover pushed his lovely smelly bone into the sack, and then scampered off to join Robin and Mary.

He forgot about his bone till the evening. Then he wanted it again. Off he went to the tool shed to have a good chew. But, alas for poor Rover, the door was shut fast! He stood and whined at it; he scraped it with his paw. But it was no use – the door wouldn't open.

'Bad luck, Rover!' said Tabby nearby. 'I suppose you've got your bone hidden in there! And you can't get at it. Dear, dear, what a pity to hide a bone in a silly place like that.'

'Well, if I can't get it, you can't either,' said Rover with a growl, and ran off.

The next day nobody went to open the tool shed to get out the tools. Poor old Rover ran to the shed a dozen times that day, but he couldn't get in, and he couldn't manage to make Robin and Mary understand that he wanted to have the door opened.

So he had to go without his bone. Tabby sat and laughed at him, and when he ran at her in a rage she jumped up on to the bookcase and sat and laughed at him there. She really was a most annoying cat.

Now, that night somebody went to the tool shed. It was midnight and everyone in the house was fast asleep. The somebody was a robber. He had come to steal as many tools as he could out of the shed!

He was very quiet, so no one heard him, not even Rover. He crept to the shed and found it locked. But he guessed that the key was not very far away, and he soon found it hung on a nail just under the roof of the shed.

He opened the door and slipped inside. He switched on his torch and looked around at the tools. They were very good ones, and kept beautifully. The man grinned. Just what he wanted! He would be able to sell them for a lot of money. He took them down quickly from their nails and put them quietly together.

I'd better slip them into a sack, in case anyone sees me on my way home, thought the robber. *I might meet the village policeman on his rounds.* He looked about for a sack and saw one on the ground. It was the one that Rover had pushed his bone into. The bone was still there, very, very smelly now. The robber picked up the sack and shook it. The bone slid to the bottom and stayed there.

The man quietly put all the tools into the sack, and then put the bundle over his shoulder. It was terribly heavy. The robber went out of the door, locked it, and hung up the key again.

He went softly to the bottom of the garden. He

put down the sack and squeezed through the hedge, pulling the sack after him.

Then he put it on his shoulder again. He walked across the field with it, but it felt so heavy that he had to put it down on the ground again.

'I believe I could drag this sack across the field more easily than I could carry it,' said the robber to himself. 'It won't matter at all if it makes a bit of a noise now, because I am well away from any of the houses.'

So he dragged the sack over the field. He came to another hedge and squeezed through it. He went down a lane, still dragging the sack, and then, when he heard footsteps, he crouched down behind a bush, listening.

It was the village policeman. He had not seen or heard the thief, and he went slowly down the lane, thinking of the hot jug of cocoa that would be waiting for him when he got home.

The man crept out from his hiding place and carried on down the lane. He came to the wood and slipped in among the dark trees. He made his way through the wood until he came to a big bank where he knew there were a lot of rabbit holes. He pushed the sack down a very big hole and pulled bracken and bramble sprays over the entrance.

I'll come and get the tools when everyone has forgotten about them, he thought. Then off he went home.

Now, in the morning, Rover ran to the tool shed early, for he knew the gardener would be there at eight o'clock to open the door. Sure enough, the man soon came along whistling. He took down the key and opened the door. Rover darted in.

But the sack was gone! Rover gave a howl of dismay – and at the same time the gardener gave a shout of surprise.

'Hey! What's happened to all the tools? They're gone!'

Tools! Who cares about tools! thought Rover. *It's my bone that is really important. Oh, tails and whiskers, wherever can it be?*

The gardener went off to tell the children's father, and Rover flew off to ask Tabby if she knew anything about his bone.

There was a great disturbance about the lost tools. The policeman was told and he came hurrying up to the house.

Nobody paid any attention at all to poor Rover and his lost bone. Tabby laughed at him.

'You needn't laugh!' said Rover. 'It was an important bone, and the robber stole that as well as the tools. I do wish I knew where it was.'

'Well, go and sniff about and see,' said Tabby, beginning to wash herself.

Rover thought that was a good idea. He ran to the tool shed. Yes, he could smell exactly where his bone had been hidden in the sack in the corner. He ran out of the shed and began to sniff around the garden, hoping to get a smell of the bone somewhere.

When he came to the hedge at the bottom he got very excited. There was the smell of bone there quite distinctly. That was where the robber had put down the sack to squeeze through the hedge. The sack smelt strongly of bone and the smell had been left on the ground beneath the hedge. Rover had a very sharp nose and he could easily smell it.

He squeezed through the hedge. He ran into the field and sniffed about. He could smell nothing till suddenly he came to the spot where the burglar had put his sack down and had begun to drag it instead. With his nose to the ground Rover followed it across the field to the second hedge, through the hedge and out into the lane.

Fancy the robber taking my bone with him in the sack such a long way! thought Rover. *It must have seemed a very fine and important bone to him. Now, here we go again – down the lane – behind this bush – down the lane again – and into the wood. Off we go – through the trees – to this bank – and, oh,* what *a strong smell of bone there is near this hole!*

Rover scraped away at the rabbit hole, sniffing his bone all the time. It was in the sack of tools, pushed down the hole. Rover couldn't get it out.

I'll go back and get Robin and Mary to help me, he thought. So he trotted back in excitement, and by pulling at Mary's skirt and Robin's trousers he managed to make them understand that he wanted them to follow him.

In great astonishment they went down the garden, through the hedge, across the field, through the second hedge, into the lane, and then into the wood to the big rabbit warren.

And there Rover showed them the sack in the rabbit hole. 'My bone's in there,' he woofed to them. 'Get it out, please.'

But Robin and Mary were not at all interested in the bone – they shouted with joy to see the tools in the sack!

'Daddy's tools! Look, they're all here! Let's take them home this very minute. Won't Daddy be pleased? Oh, you very, very clever dog, Rover, to find them for us!'

Rover trotted home beside them, sniffing his bone eagerly. What a fuss there was when the children arrived home with all the tools!

They were emptied out and counted. Yes, they were all there! 'Rover, you shall have a very big, extra-juicy bone today, for being so clever!' said Robin.

Well, that was good news. Robin rushed off to get the bone from the butcher's, and Rover put his head inside the empty sack and dragged out his beautiful old bone as well!

'I must say you were terribly clever to find all of the things that were stolen by the robber,' said Tabby in a very admiring sort of tone. Rover was extremely proud.

'Well, I am rather a clever dog, you see,' he said, 'and as you seem to have learnt that at last I'll show you that I'm a very generous dog too – you can have this bone, and I'll have the new one when it comes! And I say – have you heard? The policeman is going to hide in the wood till the robber comes to fetch the tools he hid. Then he'll be caught! I'm going to hide too. I shall have fun!'

Rover did enjoy his bone – and Tabby enjoyed the other one too. Wasn't it a good thing Rover hid his first bone in the sack?

Rabbity Ways

Rabbity Ways

THE NIGHT had been very dark, for there was no moon. Now there was a grey light creeping into the eastern sky.

Daybreak was near. Soon the owls would go home and the bats would fly back to the old barn to sleep. The oak tree that grew out of the hedgerow rustled its leaves in the chilly wind. It was a wise old tree, friendly to all creatures, and loved by a great many.

The hedgerow was old too. In it grew hawthorn, whose leaves were out early in the springtime, green fingers held up to the sun. Bramble sprays flung long arms here and there, as prickly as the wild rose that forced its way up to the sun. Ivy covered one part of the hedge, and here, in blossom time, feasted the last late flies and many beautiful red admirals.

Below was a sunny bank, for the hedgerow faced south. In summertime the birds found wild strawberries on this bank, and the primroses sometimes flowered there in the early days of January. In the ditch below there was moss growing, soft as velvet, and a few graceful ferns. It was always damp there and cool.

Near the old oak tree was a small pond, ringed round with rushes and meadowsweet. Many creatures came to drink there – from the sly red fox down to the striped yellow wasp! All the creatures in the fields around knew the pond well, and often the swallows would come and skim above it, looking for flies.

The hedgerow was in a deserted corner of the field. Nobody came there, not even the children hunting for blackberries. The farmer had forgotten to cut the hedge for years, and it had grown tall and tangled.

Sometimes the wind would bring the sound of the farmer's voice, shouting to his horses in a distant field, but usually the hedgerow knew nothing but the sound of the wind, of bird calls and pattering paws.

Many, many things had happened in and around the hedgerow. The oak tree had rustled its leaves over thousands of insects, birds and animals. Its twigs knew the difference between a squirrel's scampering paws and a bird's light hold. Its acorns had been stolen by all kinds of mice, and by the screeching jays and the hungry nuthatch.

Now it stood whispering in the cool wind of daybreak. Summer was passing over, and soon the oak leaves would lose their dark green hue and would turn brown.

The grey light in the sky became brighter. Beneath the oak tree, where the bank showed a sandy streak, a hole could just be seen. It was a rabbit's burrow. The burrow went down among the roots of the tree, exactly the size of a rabbit's body except now and again when it widened out to make passing places for two meeting rabbits. The tunnel branched off into two or three different burrows, but the rabbits had learnt every foot of them, and always knew which tunnel to take when they wanted to go to the gorse bush, to the bank or to the other side of the pond.

Out of the hole in the bank a rabbit's head appeared. Her big eyes looked through the dim grey light, her nose twitched as she sniffed the air, and her big ears listened to every sound. She wanted to go out and feed on the grass, and she had with her a young family of five rabbits, who were just getting old enough to look after themselves.

'It is safe,' she said to her young ones. 'We can go out. There is no stoat about, and the owls have all gone home.'

They trooped out of the hole. Other rabbits were in the field too, big ones and little ones, for there were many burrows there.

'Keep near the burrow,' said the mother rabbit.

'Then you will not have far to run if danger comes. I am going along the hedgerow. There is a young furze bush there and I shall feed on the juicy shoots. Keep an eye on the other rabbits, and if you see them turn so that their white bobtail shows plainly, dart into your burrow. Bobbing tails mean danger somewhere! And keep your ears pricked too – for if one of the old rabbits scents danger he will drum on the ground with his hind foot to warn us all. Then you must run as fast as you can.'

The little rabbits began to nibble the grass. They felt quite sure they could look after themselves. Their mother ran silently along the hedgerow. Suddenly she stopped and stood so still that it seemed as if she had frozen stiff. She had seen another animal coming through the hedge. It was a brown hare. As soon as the rabbit saw that it was a harmless creature, she ran on towards it. 'You scared me, cousin hare,' she said. 'Is your burrow round here?'

'Burrow!' said the hare, looking in surprise at the

rabbit, her soft eyes gleaming in the grey light. 'I have no burrow. I live above the ground.'

'But how dangerous!' said the rabbit in alarm. 'Stoats and weasels could easily find you! Do you make a nest like the birds?'

'Come with me,' said the hare. 'I will show you where I live. My home is called a form, because it is simply a dent in the ground the size and form of my body. I make it the shape of my body by lying in it, you see. I like to live alone. I should not like to live with others, as you do.'

'But it is safer,' said the rabbit, going with the hare over the field. 'I have left my young ones with the other rabbits, and they will warn them if danger is near. There is safety in numbers.'

'My ears and my nose make me safe,' said the hare. 'I can smell faraway things and hear the slightest noise. Look at my ears. They are longer than yours, cousin. See the black tips too. You have no black tips. Look at my hind legs. Yours are strong, but mine are much stronger. I can run like the wind!'

Suddenly the hare gave a great leap, and jumped many feet over the field. The rabbit was startled, but the hare called to her.

'Here is my form. I always jump like that before I go to it, so that I break my trail. Then if weasel or stoat come round they cannot follow my scent, for it breaks where I jump! Come here, cousin. I have some young ones to show you. They are only a few days old.'

The rabbit went to the hare's form. Near it were other small holes, and in each lay a young hare, a leveret, its eyes wide open, its body warmly covered with fur.

'They have made forms of their own,' said the hare proudly. 'Even when they are young they like to live alone.'

'My young ones were not like this,' said the rabbit in surprise, looking at the leverets. 'My children were born blind and deaf and had no fur on them at all. I made a special burrow for them, and blocked up the entrance to it every time I went out. I should not think of leaving them out in the open like this. It is a good thing your children are born able to see and hear, or they would certainly be eaten by an enemy!'

'They are safe enough,' said the hare. 'Now take me to your home, cousin rabbit. I would like to see your youngsters too.'

The two animals went back to the hedgerow. The hare gave another great leap when she left her form. It was a favourite trick of hers not only when leaving her home, but when she was hunted by dogs. Sometimes she would double on her tracks too, to throw off her hunters. It nearly always deceived them.

The hare was astonished to see the burrow in which the rabbits lived. 'But how do you manage about your ears?' she asked. 'Do you bend them back when you run underground? That must be very uncomfortable. It is a strange idea to tunnel in the earth. I am sure that our family were not meant to do so, or we would not have been given such long ears. It must be difficult too, to dig out all the earth.'

'No, it is easy,' said the rabbit, 'I dig with my front paws and shovel out the earth with my hind paws. See, cousin, there are my children feeding over there.'

The hare was looking at the young rabbits in the light of the dawn when a curious noise came to her long ears. It was a drumming sound, and it seemed to the hare as if the ground were quivering under her feet. The mother rabbit called to her young ones at once.

'Come here! There is danger about! That is the old rabbit drumming with his hind feet to warn us. Come, cousin, you must hide in our burrow too.'

The young rabbits lifted their heads when they heard the drumming. Then they saw all the other rabbits running in every direction to their holes, their white bobtails showing clearly. In seconds the young ones were off too, scampering to their hole. Not a rabbit was to be seen when the old red fox came slinking by. The hare had gone too – but not down the burrow.

My legs are safer than a burrow! she thought to herself. *I shall run, not hide! No fox can catch* me!

Poor hare! thought the rabbit. *She ought to dig a burrow, then she would be safe. The fox will surely get her.*

But the fox went hungry that morning!

Binkle's Tail

Binkle's Tail

ONCE THERE was a guinea pig called Binkle. He lived in a cage just outside Jinky the gnome's front door, and he was very proud of himself.

'My whiskers are fine, my fur is soft, and my ears are pretty!' he said to himself. 'No wonder all Jinky's visitors come and talk to me!'

But one day Panikin the pixie said something that gave Binkle a terrible fright.

'Whatever you do, Jinky, don't let anyone hold Binkle up by his tail. If you do, his eyes will fall out!' he said solemnly.

'Oh! Oh! Oh!' squeaked poor Binkle, hiding

himself in a corner. 'I do hope nobody would do such a cruel thing!'

Jinky the gnome and Panikin the pixie laughed loudly and Binkle couldn't think what they were laughing at. When they had gone he began thinking very hard.

Just suppose someone did come and hold me up by my tail! he thought. *How terrible it would be! I wonder what my tail is like?* He tried to see it, but he was such a plump little guinea pig that he couldn't see anything beyond his humpy back.

'It must be rather a long tail,' he said sadly. 'Perhaps Panikin was afraid some rude person would swing me upside down by it. Oh dear! What shall I do?'

The more he thought about it, the more he felt afraid. At last he decided to run away that night, go to Snip the tailor, and ask him to cut his tail right off. *Then no one can hold me up by it!* thought Binkle.

So that night, out he scampered and ran down the road to Snip the tailor.

Snip was sitting making a coat for a brownie. 'Hello!' he said in surprise. 'What do you want, Binkle?'

'Please would you cut my tail off?' begged Binkle. 'I'm afraid someone will hold me up by it, and then my eyes would drop out, you know.'

Snip stared at him, and smiled. 'I'm terribly sorry,' he said, 'but I'm afraid my scissors couldn't cut off your tail; they're not the right sort. Go and ask Periwinkle the dressmaker. She's got a pair of brand-new scissors!'

'Thank you,' said Binkle and off he scampered. As he went he heard Snip laughing, and he couldn't think what he was laughing at. He climbed the hill to Periwinkle's.

'I want my tail cut off, in case someone holds me up by it and makes my eyes fall out,' explained Binkle. 'Snip said you'd got a new pair of scissors.'

'So I have. But I'm afraid they wouldn't cut your tail off, Binkle,' said Periwinkle. 'Go and ask Pippit the draper. He's got lots of scissors there.'

'Thank you,' said Binkle, and ran off as quickly as he could. As he went, he heard Periwinkle laughing, and he couldn't think what she was laughing at.

Pippit the draper was just shutting up shop when Binkle came panting up.

'Why, Binkle!' said Pippit. 'Why are you out so late?'

'I'm dreadfully worried about my tail,' said Binkle. 'If I'm held up by it, my eyes will drop out. Periwinkle said you could cut it off, as you have lots of scissors.'

'So I have,' said Pippit, laughing. 'But they're all much too small. Why don't you go to the Simple Witch down in the valley? She's got a pair of magic scissors.'

Binkle hurried to the witch's cottage, wondering why Pippit had laughed, and asked for her help. 'Pippit said you had some magic scissors. It won't hurt, will it?'

'Oh, no, Binkle, it won't hurt you at all!' chuckled the Simple Witch.

She picked up a pair of big shiny scissors. Binkle turned his back to her and waited nervously. Snip! Snap! he heard, but he felt nothing at all.

'There you are!' said the witch. 'You haven't any tail to worry about now, Binkle!'

'Oh, thank you very much indeed!' said Binkle, and ran home, full of delight.

As he went, he heard the witch laughing and laughing, and he couldn't think what she was laughing at. He cuddled himself up in his little cage, and felt very happy.

Now I'm quite safe, he thought. *My eyes will never drop out. I wonder what Jinky will say. Won't he be pleased to think no one can ever hold me up by my tail!*

Binkle soon fell fast asleep. When he woke the next day he tried to look over his plump shoulder to check that his tail wasn't there. But, of course, he was much too fat.

Just then, Jinky came whistling down the garden. But, dear me, he didn't seem to notice anything new about Binkle at all, and he couldn't think why the little guinea pig kept turning his back on him. 'What's the matter, Binkle?' he asked at last.

'I've had my tail cut off,' said Binkle proudly, 'so that no one can hold me up by it and make my eyes fall out! The Simple Witch did it with her magic scissors!'

To his surprise Jinky began to laugh and laugh, and Binkle couldn't think what he was laughing at. 'What's the matter?' he asked, quite offended.

'Oh, Binkle – hee, hee, hee – it's so funny – ha, ha – you never had a tail at all – ho, ho, ho! Guinea pigs don't have tails, you silly!' Jinky said, laughing loudly.

And then Binkle knew why Snip and Periwinkle, Pippit and the Simple Witch had all laughed so loudly the night before. Poor Binkle!

The Cat Without Whiskers

The Cat Without Whiskers

INKY WAS a black cat with the finest white whiskers in the street. He was a handsome cat, with sharp ears and a long thick tail that looked like a snake when he waved it to and fro. He had a white mark under his chin, which the children called his bib, and he washed it three times a day, so that it was always like snow.

Inky was plump, for he was the best ratter and mouser in the town and never lacked a good dinner. When he sat on the wall washing himself he was a fine sight, for his glossy fur gleamed in the sun and his whiskers stuck out each side of his face like white wires.

'I'm the finest-looking cat in the town,' said Inky

proudly, and he looked scornfully down at the tabby in the garden below, and the white cat washing itself on a windowsill nearby. 'Nobody is as good-looking as me!'

Then a little boy came by, and when he saw the big black cat sitting up on the wall he shouted up at him, laughing, 'Hello, Whiskers!'

Inky was offended. His name wasn't Whiskers. It was Inky. A little girl heard what the boy said and she laughed. 'That's a good name for him,' she said. 'He's a very whiskery cat. Whiskers!'

Everyone thought it a funny name, and soon Inky was being called Whiskers all day long, even by the cats and dogs around. This made him really very angry.

It's a horrid silly name, he thought crossly, *and it's rude of people to call me that. They don't call that nice old gentleman with the beard 'Whiskers', do they? And they don't shout 'Nosy' at that boy with the big nose. I shan't answer them when they call me Whiskers!*

So he didn't – but it wasn't any good, for everyone

shouted 'Whiskers! Whiskers!' as soon as they saw Inky's wonderful whiskers.

Inky thought hard. 'I shall get rid of my whiskers,' he said to himself. 'Yes, I shall start a new fashion for cats. We won't have whiskers. After all, men shave every morning, and people think that is a good idea. I will shave my whiskers off, and then no one will call me Whiskers.'

He told his idea to wise old Shelly-Back the tortoise. Shelly-Back listened and pulled at the grass he was eating.

'It is best not to meddle with things you have been given,' he said. 'You will be sorry.'

'No, I shan't,' said Inky. 'My whiskers are no use to me that I can see – I shall shave them off!'

Well, he slipped into the bathroom at his home early the next morning and found the thing his master called a razor. In an instant Inky had shaved off his beautiful whiskers. They were gone. He was no longer a whiskery cat.

He looked at himself in the glass. He did look a bit strange – but at any rate no one would now shout 'Whiskers' after him. He slipped down the stairs and out into the garden. He jumped on the wall in the sun.

The milkman came by and looked at him. He did not shout 'Whiskers!' as he usually did. He stared in rather a puzzled way and said nothing at all. Then a young boy came by delivering papers, and he didn't shout 'Whiskers!' either.

Inky was pleased. At last he had got rid of his horrid name. He sat in the sun, purring, and soon his friends gathered round him. There was Tabby from next door, the white cat Snowball, Shelly-Back the tortoise, who looked up at him from the lawn, and the old dog Rover, who never chased cats.

'What's the matter with you this morning, Inky?' asked Snowball, puzzled. 'You look different.'

'His whiskers are gone,' said Tabby, startled. 'How strange!'

'How did you lose them?' asked Rover.

'I shaved them off,' Inky said proudly. 'I am starting a new fashion for cats. Grown-up men shave their whiskers off each day, don't they? Well, why should cats have whiskers? Don't you think I look much smarter now?'

Everyone stared at Inky, but nobody said a word. They all thought Inky looked dreadful without his whiskers.

'You'll soon see everyone following my fashion of no whiskers,' said Inky. 'It's much more comfortable. Whiskers always get in my way when I'm washing my face, but now I can wash it as smoothly as anything. Look!' He washed his face with his paw. Certainly it looked easier to do it without whiskers. But the older animals shook their heads.

'Whiskers must be some use or we wouldn't have them,' said Tabby.

'Well, what use are they?' said Inky.

But nobody was clever enough to think of anything to say in answer to that. One by one they slipped off to their homes to dinner, quite determined that they were not going to shave off their whiskers, whatever Inky did.

Now, that night Inky felt very hungry. He had been late for tea that afternoon and a stray dog had gone into his garden and eaten up the plate of fish and milk that his mistress had put out for him. Inky was annoyed.

Never mind, he thought to himself. *I'll go hunting tonight. I'll catch a few mice and perhaps a rat or two. I know a good place in the hedge at the bottom of the garden. I'll hide on one side of it and wait for the night animals to come out.*

So off he went when darkness came and crouched down on one side of the hedge. Soon he heard the pitter-pattering of little mice feet. Inky stiffened and kept quite still. In a moment he would squeeze through the hedge and pounce on those foolish mice.

He took a step forward. His paw was like velvet and made no noise. He pushed his head into a hole in the hedge – then his body – but alas for Inky! His body was too big for the hole, and the hedge creaked as he tried to get through. The mice heard the noise and shot off into their holes. Not one was left.

'Bother!' said Inky crossly. 'I'll wait again. I believe that old rat has a run here somewhere. I'd like to catch him!'

So he waited – and, sure enough, the big rat ran silently by the hedge. Inky heard him and began to creep towards him, but his fat body brushed against some leaves and the rat heard and fled.

Inky was astonished. Usually he could hunt marvellously without making a single sound. Why was it that his body seemed so clumsy tonight? Why did he brush against things and make rustling noises? It was most annoying.

And then suddenly he knew the reason why. Although he hadn't thought about it, his fine whiskers had always helped him to hunt. They had stretched out each side of his face, and were just about the width of his body. He had known that if he could get his head and whiskers through a hole without touching anything, his body would go through easily too without a sound.

It was my whiskers that helped my body to know if it could go easily and silently through the holes and between leaves, thought Inky in despair. *Of course! Why didn't I think of that before? They were just the right width for my body, and I knew quite well if I touched anything with my whiskers that my body would also touch it and make a noise – and so I would go another way!*

Inky was quite right. His whiskers had helped him in his hunting. Now he would not be able to hunt well, for he would never know if his body could squeeze through gaps and holes. He would always be making rustling, crackling noises with leaves and twigs. He would never catch anything. Poor Inky!

You can guess that Inky was always waiting for his mistress to put out his dinner after that – for he hardly ever caught a mouse or rat now. He grew much thinner, and he hid himself away, for he was ashamed to think that he had shaved off the things that had been so useful to him.

A new fashion indeed! thought Inky. *I was mad! If only I had my lovely whiskers again I wouldn't mind being called 'Whiskers' a hundred times a day. My life is spoilt. I shall never be able to hunt again.*

He was a sad and unhappy cat, ashamed to talk to anyone except wise old Shelly-Back the tortoise. One day he told Shelley-Back why he was unhappy. Shelly-Back looked at him closely and laughed.

'Go and sit up on the wall in the sun and see what happens,' he said to Inky. 'You'll find your troubles are not so big as you thought they were.'

In surprise Inky jumped up on the wall and sat there in the sun. The milkman came by with his cart. He looked up.

'Hello, Whiskers!' he shouted. 'Good old Whiskers!'

Inky nearly fell off the wall in astonishment. What? He was called Whiskers again even if he had shaved them off? But silly old Inky had quite forgotten something. What had he forgotten?

He had forgotten that whiskers grow again like hair. His whiskers had grown out fine and long and strong and white – and he had been so miserable that he hadn't even noticed. Silly old Whiskers!

He was happy when he found that he had them again. He sat and purred so loudly that Shelly-Back really thought there was an aeroplane flying somewhere near! It sounded just like it.

And now Inky can hunt again, and is the best mouser in the town. He has grown plump and handsome, and his whiskers are finer than ever. He loves to hear himself called Whiskers now. So if you see him up on the wall, black and shining, don't say 'Hello, Inky!' – shout 'Good old Whiskers!' and he'll purr like a kettle on the boil!

It's Nice to Have
a Friend

It's Nice to Have
a Friend

TIBS WAS a farm cat. She was a little tabby, with fine big whiskers and a nice long tail.

Punch was the farm dog. He was a big collie with a bushy tail and a very loud bark. He didn't like cats one little bit and Tibs didn't like dogs.

Tibs hardly ever went near Punch unless he was tied up, because she knew he would chase her, and Punch was always on the watch for her so that he could tear after her and send her flying up to the top of the wall hissing and spitting. Then he would bark the place down!

Now, one day when Punch was tied up he came out

into the yard on his long chain to sniff at a garden roller that somebody had left there. He walked round it – and somehow or other his chain got twisted, and he couldn't get back to his kennel. There he was, held tightly by the garden roller, his chain pulling at his neck.

Punch pulled at it. He rolled over to try to get it loose – and all that happened was that he twisted his chain so much that it almost choked him!

He couldn't bark; he could only make a whine or a growl. So nobody heard him and nobody came to help him. He choked and struggled, but his chain was too tightly twisted round the heavy garden roller for him to get free.

Only Tibs, the farm cat, heard the noises he was making. She jumped on to the top of the wall and looked at poor Punch. What peculiar noises! What was the matter with him?

'Tibs!' croaked Punch. 'Help me. I'm choking.'

Tibs jumped down and had a look. No, she couldn't

help him. She didn't know anything about chains! But she was sorry for Punch, and she thought of something else. She ran to the farmhouse and mewed loudly.

Mrs Straws, the farmer's wife, came to the door. 'What is it?' she said. Tibs ran a little way away and looked back. The farmer's wife followed her – and then she too heard the strange noises that Punch was making out in the yard.

She went to see what they were – and in a minute or two she had undone the chain, untwisted it, patted poor Punch and given him a long drink of water!

Punch looked at Tibs on the wall. 'Thank you,' he said. 'You can come down and sit near me. I shall never chase you again. You saved me from choking.'

But Tibs didn't really trust him. She would never come down from the wall. Still, they had many a talk together and that was nice for both of them.

Then one day Tibs didn't come. She didn't come for three days, and then she told Punch why.

'I've got four little kittens,' she told him proudly.

'They're my very own. They're in the kitchen. But I do wish the children would leave them alone. They are always pulling them about, and it worries me.'

The next day Tibs looked even more worried. 'Bobby took one of my kittens and dropped it,' she said. 'I'm going to take them away from the kitchen. I shall put them in the barn.'

So she took each of her kittens by the neck and carried them one by one to a corner of the barn. But the children found them there and took them back to the kitchen again. They were like live toys to them, and they wanted to play with them!

Tibs was unhappy. She liked the children and she didn't want to scratch them. 'But what am I to do, Punch?' she said. 'One of my kittens has a bad leg because Bobby squeezed it too hard yesterday. I wish I could think of somewhere else to take them.'

Punch listened, his big head on one side. 'I know a place where nobody would ever find them,' he said. 'But I don't think you'd like it. It's a place where nobody would ever, ever look.'

'Where?' asked Tibs.

'Here in my kennel!' said Punch. 'There's plenty of good warm straw – and plenty of room for you and your kittens at the back. I promise not to sit on you. I'll be very, very careful. You were good to me once – now let me be kind to you!'

Tibs thought about it. Did she trust Punch or didn't she? He was a dog. She was a cat. She didn't know if they could really be friends. Still – she would try!

So, when nobody was about, Tibs carried each of her kittens by its neck all the way from the kitchen to the yard where the kennel was. One by one she laid the little things in the warm straw at the back. Then she settled down on them herself, purring happily.

Punch was very good. He didn't even let his tail rest on the kittens, and he gave them all the room he could. He even licked them when Tibs wasn't there, and when one of them patted his nose he was surprised and delighted.

The children looked all over the place for the kittens. They called and called Tibs. But she didn't come. She wasn't going to give her hiding place away! Her kittens were safe and happy now. Punch sat in his kennel, so that nobody could even peep in. Aha! Look where you like, Bobby and Betty, you won't find the kittens!

'It's nice to have a friend,' purred Tibs. 'Nobody knows where I am. Keep my secret, Punch.'

He will, of course – and we certainly won't tell Bobby and Betty, will we?

Hurrah for the Pepperpot!

Hurrah for the Pepperpot!

TWO FAMILIES of mice lived in the old kitchen. One was Mrs Whisker Mouse's family and the other was Mrs Furry Mouse's.

They sometimes used to visit one another when the kitchen cat was not about. When Mrs Whisker's youngest mouse, Paddy-Paws, had a party, all Mrs Furry's children were most excited.

You should have seen the way that Mrs Furry dressed them up! The boys had red trousers and blue coats, the girls had tiny blue skirts and little shawls. They really looked most amusing.

They set off to the party. Mrs Furry first of all put

her nose out of her hole to make quite sure the cat wasn't in the kitchen. She sniffed. She could smell no cat. But she could smell cheese up on the table! A meal was laid there for the farmer. Mrs Furry made up her mind that she would have a look at that cheese when the party was over. She set off across the kitchen with her little family.

The party was great fun. There were cheese cakes, bacon rind sandwiches and potato peel pies. After the meal they all played games, and they squeaked and squealed so loudly that they didn't hear the big kitchen cat come stealing into the kitchen.

But he heard their squeaks and squeals! He blinked his big green eyes and sat himself down in a dark corner to wait until the mouse family came by.

When the party was over, Mrs Furry and her family came quietly out of Mrs Whisker's hole. 'We'll just go up on to the table and see if we can nibble a bit of cheese!' whispered Mrs Furry to her four children. 'Come along! We can climb up the tablecloth. It nearly touches the ground at the corners of the table.'

So they all ran to the tablecloth and were up it in an instant! The cat was cross. It had hoped they were going straight to their hole. Then it could have caught them.

Now, as the mice were climbing up to the table, Mrs Furry caught a smell of cat. She was frightened at once. Oh dear, where could the cat be? She stood on the table and sniffed and sniffed.

'That cat is somewhere about!' she whispered to her four children. 'Keep up here with me. Don't move! Oh, if only I knew whether the cat is over there – or by the sink – or sitting just by our own hole! It is so dark that I can't see a thing.' The five mice sat as still as could be. So did the cat. They were all listening for each other. But nobody made a sound. Not one single sound.

So the cat didn't know where the mice were and the mice didn't know where the cat was.

'Mother, surely we haven't got to stay here all

night!' whispered one of the little mice. 'Why, when daylight comes we shall be easily seen.'

'Oh dear, if only I knew where that cat is!' said Mrs Furry. 'How could I find out?'

She ran a few steps over the tablecloth and bumped into something hard. It was the pepperpot. And then Mrs Furry had a really splendid idea! She went back to her little family.

'Get out your hankies and bury your noses in them,' she whispered. 'I'm going to shake the pepperpot as hard as I can, all round the edge of the table. Then, if the cat is anywhere near, he will sneeze loudly when the pepper gets up his nose. But you mustn't sneeze and give away where we are – so get out your hankies!'

Then all the little mice got out their hankies and put their sharp little noses into them. Mrs Furry picked up the pepperpot and ran to the edge of the table with it.

Shake-shake-shake! She emptied a whole lot of pepper on to the floor. Then she went to the other side.

Shake-shake-shake! Down went some more yellow pepper, flying through the air. Shake-shake-shake! Shake-shake-shake!

And then a most tremendous sneeze came up from the floor! The cat had got some pepper up his nose and he simply could not stop himself from sneezing!

'A-TISHOO!' he went, 'A-TISHOO!'

Mrs Furry scampered back to her family. 'The cat is over by the sink!' she whispered. 'Come along, slip down this side of the table, and run for your hole!'

Down they all went and scampered across the kitchen as fast as they could go. The cat heard them, but another enormous sneeze came and nearly took his head off.

'A-TISHOO!' he went, just as the last mouse squeezed down the hole.

'Hurrah for the pepperpot!' cried Mrs Furry.

And 'Hurrah, hurrah!' cried all the little mice.

Adventure in
the Woods

Adventure in the Woods

ONE BEAUTIFUL moonlit night Johnny couldn't sleep. He sat up in bed and saw the moonlight streaming over his bed. Shadow, his lovely sheepdog, was lying at the foot on an old rug.

When Johnny sat up, Shadow awoke. He lifted his big head, cocked his ears and looked at his master.

'Shadow! I can't sleep!' said Johnny. 'It's too beautiful a night to waste. Let's go for a walk on the hills, shall we? Just you and I together?'

'Woof!' said Shadow in a low voice, for he knew they must not wake Johnny's father and mother. The boy slid out of bed and dressed quickly. Then he and Shadow crept out of the room and were soon in the farmyard.

The moonlight shone down and everything could be clearly seen. The ducks were on the pond, quacking, and Jessie, the farmyard dog, lay outside her kennel awake.

'Where are you going?' she asked Shadow in surprise.

'Out for a walk with Johnny!' said Shadow joyously, wagging his plumy tail. 'I've never done this before – gone out in the moonlight. I've often wondered why people don't do it – the world is lovely and pale and quiet then. We're going out on the hills.'

They were soon there. The sheep lay dotted on the hillside half asleep. Rafe and Tucker greeted Shadow as he and Johnny passed them.

'Hallo! You're out late, aren't you?'

'Off for a walk with Johnny,' said Shadow proudly. 'Where are Bob and Dandy, the other dogs?'

'Bob's over there, outside the shepherd's hut,' said

Tucker. 'I don't know where Dandy is. He went off early this morning and hasn't come back. You know what he is for wandering away. Still, we're pretty busy with the sheep just now – I'm surprised he hasn't turned up.'

The big sheepdog wagged his tail at Shadow and then lay down quietly again. Johnny patted Tucker and Rafe and went up the hill, Shadow close beside him.

Shadow wondered where Dandy had got to. It was strange that he hadn't returned before night. He ran beside Johnny, sniffing at all the smells they passed, enjoying the moonlight walk.

Then suddenly he heard a faint and faraway sound. It was so distant that at first Shadow didn't think he had heard anything. Then it came again. The big sheepdog stood still, his ears cocked well up.

'Come on, old boy,' said Johnny. 'What are you standing there like that for? There's no one about tonight. Come on, I want to get over the hill.'

Shadow trotted on again. Then, on the wind, there came that faint sound once more. Shadow stood still and listened, puzzled.

'Shadow! Whatever's the matter with you?' shouted back Johnny impatiently. 'I shan't take you out at night again if you don't keep up with me.'

Shadow ran to his little master once more, but his ears were listening all the time. And when the wind blew around him again, bringing with it that faint sound, Shadow knew what it was.

It was the faraway whine of a dog in pain. And that dog must be Dandy!

Shadow looked at Johnny. The boy was running down the other side of the hill. The moon was so bright that Shadow could even see the pattern on his sweater. Johnny was all right. He knew his way back. Shadow felt that he really must go and see what had happened to Dandy.

He stood and barked loudly to Johnny, hoping that the boy would understand. Then he turned and ran quickly down the hill again, into the valley, and made for the woods that lay on the next hill to the east.

Johnny was puzzled when Shadow disappeared. He called and whistled, but Shadow was out of hearing. The boy went back a little way to see if the sheepdog was rabbiting, but there was no sign of him.

It's too bad of Shadow, thought Johnny vexed. *He always keeps up with me when he is out for a walk. Why should he leave me? I won't take him out again!*

He went on by himself, wondering where Shadow was. The sheepdog was far away by that time, running tirelessly on his strong legs. He came to the wood, and then the wailing sound he had heard came again, much louder because it was nearer.

It is *Dandy!* thought Shadow. *Poor old Dandy. What can have happened?*

He ran swiftly towards the sound and came to where Dandy was lying in the wood. Shadow ran up to him and barked. 'What's up? Why don't you come home?'

Dandy answered with a pitiful whine. Then Shadow saw that the poor dog had his foot caught in a steel trap. It had been set for rabbits, and was a cruel thing with steel teeth that bit into an animal's leg and held it fast. Dandy hadn't seen it and had put his foot right into it. Now he was held tight and was in great pain. The trap was too heavy for him to move or he might have dragged it along with him.

Shadow tore at it with his teeth, but Dandy stopped him. 'That's no use,' he said. 'I know these traps. I can only get my foot out if someone opens the trap, and only people know how to do that. You can't open it.'

'I'll go and fetch someone who can,' said Shadow, and he looked anxiously at Dandy, who had lain his head down wearily on his good paw. The dog was tired out with pain.

Shadow ran off, his heart beating fast because he ran so swiftly. He must get help for Dandy. He must not let him suffer one minute more pain than he could help. How his poor foot must hurt him! How wicked those steel traps were!

Shadow ran back to the farm. Johnny had got back now and was in his bedroom, about to take off his sweater. Shadow padded into the room and went up to him. But Johnny pushed him away.

'Shadow, I don't want you! You left me tonight. The moon might have gone in and left me in the dark, and I might have got lost. I am ashamed of you. Go away.'

Shadow's heart sank when he heard Johnny talk to him like that. He licked his hand, but the boy took it away. Then Shadow took hold of his sleeve and gave it a gentle tug. That meant, 'Please come with me!'

'If you think I'm going to take you out for a walk again, you're wrong,' said Johnny crossly. 'And I don't want you to sleep on my bed tonight. If you're going to run off and leave me when I want you, I don't want you to sleep with me.'

Shadow felt as if his heart was breaking. Johnny had never said such a thing to him before. The dog pressed himself close to the boy and licked wherever he could. His tail drooped down. Then he took the corner of Johnny's sweater in his mouth and tugged it again.

Johnny looked down into the soft brown eyes. Shadow was speaking to him as clearly as could be. 'Come with me,' his eyes were saying.

Johnny was puzzled. 'Well, I'll come,' he said at last. 'But if it's just for nothing, I shall be cross with you.'

Shadow took Johnny into the moonlit farmyard once more, and then took the path to the woods. Johnny followed, more and more puzzled. But when at last he stood looking down at Dandy he knew why Shadow had run from him, and why the dog had tugged at his sweater!

'Oh, Dandy! What's wrong?' cried Johnny, and he knelt down beside the tired dog. The moonlight glinted on the bright trap, and Johnny gave a cry of dismay.

'You've got your foot in a trap! Oh, Dandy, you poor poor thing! How long have you been here? Oh, how am I to open the trap?'

Dandy whined a little. He was so tired out with pain that he could hardly lift his head. Shadow pulled at the trap. Johnny looked at it carefully and saw how to open it. He must put his foot on one part, and then drag open the steel teeth.

The boy tried – and at last the cruel teeth parted, and there was Dandy's foot, free, but crushed and bleeding. The dog did not know at first that his foot was free, for it still hurt him terribly.

'Take your foot out before the trap shuts again!' cried Johnny. And Dandy painfully moved his poor foot. He stood up on three legs, holding his wounded foot high. It still hurt, though with a different pain now. But at any rate he was free. He could get away from that horrible steel thing that had held him prisoner!

The three of them went home slowly, for Dandy was tired.

Johnny woke his father and the two of them gently bathed and bound up the hurt foot.

'Dandy, if you *will* go off hunting by yourself like this, you *must* learn to look out for traps!' said the farmer. 'Poor creature, you won't be much use looking after the sheep for a week or two. But your foot will mend. Go and sleep in the yard with Jessie the farm dog tonight.'

Dandy trotted off on three legs. He licked Shadow as he went.

'Thank you,' he said. 'You're a good friend. No wonder Johnny loves you best in the world!'

But that's just what he doesn't do! thought Shadow sadly as he lay down by the kitchen fire. *Johnny has said tonight that he doesn't want me on his bed. He is angry because I left him. But how could I leave Dandy in pain?*

Johnny wondered where Shadow was. He was now in bed, waiting for the sheepdog to come and jump up on his feet. But Shadow didn't come.

Surely he doesn't think I'm still cross with him! thought Johnny.

He went to the kitchen – and there was Shadow by the fire, ears and tail well down. 'Shadow!' cried Johnny. 'Come here! I want you on my bed. I think you're a good clever dog to find poor Dandy like that and fetch me to him. I understand why you left me now – and you were quite right. I'm sorry I was cross. Come here, Shadow!'

And Shadow came gladly, whining a little and licking the boy's bare legs. He lay down happily on Johnny's bed, nibbling the boy's toes with love. Nothing in the world mattered so long as Johnny wanted him close!

Dozymouse and Flittermouse

Dozymouse and Flittermouse

THE LITTLE dormouse knew the hedgerow from end to end. He had lived there for two summers and winters, and he knew every creature that ran beneath the hedge, perched in the bushes, or flew in the air above. His big black eyes watched everything.

He was a small tawny-coloured mouse, with a long thickly furred tail. He could run and he could climb, and even the oak tree knew him well, for he had many times run up the trunk and along the branches to talk to the squirrel there.

At first the red squirrel had thought the dormouse was a tiny squirrel, for he had such a furry tail, such large, bright eyes, and the squirrel-like habit of sitting upright with a nut in his paws.

'A squirrel!' said the dormouse in surprise. 'No, not I! I'm one of the mouse family. I've lots of names – dormouse is my right name, but I'm often called Sleepymouse and sometimes Dozymouse. I sleep very soundly, you know.'

'Well, I know a strange creature called Flittermouse,' said the red squirrel. 'You must be a cousin of his.'

'I've never heard of him,' said the dormouse. 'Where does he live?'

'He lives inside the oak tree,' said the squirrel. 'Come and peep.'

The dormouse looked into the hollow trunk of the old oak tree. He saw something black there, hanging upside down, perfectly still.

'Why,' he said, 'it's a bat! I thought you said it was a flittermouse.'

'Well, so it is, isn't it?' said the squirrel. 'It's like

a little brown mouse with big black wings that flit about in the dusk – a flittermouse.'

The dormouse woke up the bat. It stretched itself and unfolded its webby wings. It had hung itself up by its hook-like thumbs.

'Is it night-time?' asked the bat in a thin, squeaky voice. 'Are there many flies and beetles about?'

'It is indeed getting dark,' answered the dormouse. 'But, please tell me something. The squirrel says you must be a cousin of mine. But how can you be a mouse if you have wings? You must be a bird.'

'No, no,' said the bat, flying out of the tree and perching very awkwardly beside the dormouse. 'I am no bird. Look at me. I haven't a feather on my back. I don't lay eggs either.'

'What are your wings made of then?' asked the dormouse.

'Look!' said the bat, and he stretched out one of his strange wings. 'The bones of my fingers have grown enormously long, and I have grown black skin over them to make wings. Isn't it a good idea?'

'I wish *I* could do that,' said the dormouse. 'How do you grow your fingers so long?'

But he received no answer for the bat was off and away into the air, darting here and there easily and swiftly. He caught some evening beetles and popped each one into a little pouch he had by his tail. Then he feasted on them, giving high, little squeaks of delight as he flew.

The dormouse watched him in envy. He liked flies when he could catch them, though he found it better to feed on nuts or grain, for fly-food darted away, and nuts and grain kept still. He peeped inside the oak tree where the bat had hidden. It smelt strongly of bat.

'I'm glad I don't smell like that,' he said to himself, as he ran quickly down the tree. He stopped at the bottom, and sniffed in every direction. He was always on the lookout for weasels, who loved a feast of dormouse.

There was no enemy near, so the dormouse ran to

his summer nest to tell his wife to come out and hunt. He went to the hedgerow and clambered up the brambles. A little way up was his nest, in which he had had several families of tiny dormice that summer. Now the last of them had gone, and all were running about on their own. The dormouse sometimes met them in the hedgerow, but most of them had grown so big that he hardly knew them.

The nest was well made, tucked into the bramble stems. The dormouse had decided to make it of the bark from the stems of the old honeysuckle that grew further down the hedgerow. He had torn it off in long strips, and he and his wife had made their nest with the pieces. Inside they had lined the nest with leaves, so that it was cosy and warm. It was so well hidden that not even the rabbits guessed where it was.

In the daytime the dormice hid in their nest and slept soundly. At night they woke up and went hunting for food. They loved nuts, berries and grain, and if they chanced upon a fat caterpillar they would take that too. As the summer went by they grew fatter and fatter, and the nest shook with their weight!

'When the autumn comes we must build a nest underground,' said the dormice. 'This one will be too easily seen when the bramble leaves fall.'

When October came the dormice were so fat and round that there really was not enough room for them both in their nest. The nights became chilly. The dormice felt more and more sleepy.

So they hunted about and at last found a little tunnel going right down among the roots of the hedgerow, quite a long way underground. They took some moss down the hole and arranged it in a little round place among the roots. They would be warm and comfortable there, far away from any enemy.

'Now we must take plenty of food down to our new nest,' said the dormouse to his wife. 'We might wake up on a warm winter's day and feel hungry.'

It was while they were hunting for food that they heard the bat calling to them. The dormouse once again climbed the oak tree and looked at the strange little bat clinging clumsily to the branch.

'I want to say goodbye,' said the bat. 'It's getting cold now, and I am going to hide myself away for the winter.'

'We are just doing the same!' said the dormouse in surprise. 'We have made a nice nest far underground among the hedgerow roots, and we are hoarding up some food in case we wake up on a warm winter's day and want a meal.'

'I don't do that,' said the bat. 'My food wouldn't keep like yours. It would go bad, because I eat only beetles and flies. But if I wake up it will be such a warm spell that a few flies are sure to be about too, and I shall catch them. I am going to fly to an old cave I know across the fields. A great many of my relations will be there – big bats and little bats, long-eared bats and short-eared ones, and little common bats like myself.'

'Do you make a nest?' asked the dormouse.

'Of course not!' said the bat. 'No bat ever makes a nest! We shall all hang ourselves up by our hooked thumbs, upside down, cover ourselves with our wings and soon we will be fast asleep.'

'What do you do with your young ones if you don't make a nest to keep them in?' asked the dormouse in surprise.

'Oh, we keep our little ones cuddled against our fur, even when we fly in the air,' answered the bat. 'They cling tightly and never fall. Well, dormouse, I hope I see you well and fat in the springtime. You look fat enough now!'

'So do you!' said the little dormouse.

'Ah, it's a good thing to get fat before the long, hungry wintertime!' said the bat. 'We shall get through the cold days comfortably then. Well, goodbye.'

'Just come and see my nest before you go,' begged the dormouse.

'I can't,' said the bat impatiently. 'Haven't you seen my knees? They turn backwards instead of forwards, so that I can't walk. I am only made for flying!' He rose into the air and darted swiftly away.

'Goodbye, little flittermouse!' called the dormouse, and then, feeling a touch of frost in the air, he ran quickly to his hole. His small, fat wife was waiting for him. Without a word they curled up together in the warm moss and fell asleep. They became as cold as ice, they seemed not to breathe, so soundly asleep were they – but a warm night would awaken them, and then they would feast eagerly on their little store of nuts in the roots of the hedgerow.

Granny's Kittens

Granny's Kittens

'DAISY, PUT on your hat and go to Granny's,' said Mummy. 'She has some nice homemade sweets for my sale of work, and I told her you would fetch them.'

'Oh, yes, Mummy – I'll go now,' said Daisy, pleased. 'Granny's cat has got kittens, you know, and I shall see them, if she hasn't given them all away yet. Oh, Mummy, I do so wish we could have one.'

But Mother didn't like cats, and she shook her head. 'No, dear. Don't keep asking me that. Now hurry up and go.'

Daisy soon got to Granny's. She kissed the old lady's soft, wrinkled face and then asked about the kittens.

'They've all gone but one, the prettiest of the lot,' said Granny. 'It's the little white one. Now where is the little kitten? Call it.'

'Kitty, kitty, kitty!' called Daisy, but the kitten didn't come. Daisy looked everywhere for it. She looked under the bed, under the couch and out in the garden. Only Tabby, the big mother cat, was there, sitting washing herself on the wall.

'Where's your white kitten?' asked Daisy, but Tabby took no notice at all. Daisy thought her kittens were much nicer than she was. Tabby never played at all.

'I can't find the kitten, Granny,' said Daisy sadly. 'I'm sorry I can't, because I'm sure next time I come it will be gone.'

'I'm sorry you can't find it,' said Granny. 'It's always hiding away somewhere. Now you had better go back, darling, because it is getting late.'

'What about the homemade sweets for Mummy's sale, Granny?' asked Daisy. 'She said I was to bring them back.'

'Oh, yes,' said Granny. 'I've got everything ready in this basket. I've put the boxes of sweets at the very bottom, and above them I have put some knitted gloves and hot-water bottle covers I have made for Mummy's sale too. The basket is quite light, so you can easily carry it.'

Daisy picked it up. She kissed Granny goodbye and went down the path. Granny had given her one of her homemade bits of toffee, and Daisy sucked at it as she went.

The basket was quite heavy. It dragged at Daisy's arm, and she took it in the other hand. 'Dear me,' she said, 'it feels very heavy, although Granny said it was light. I shall be tired when I get home!'

She found her mother when she got home. She put the basket on the table, and Mother kissed her. 'You're a good, helpful little girl,' she said, 'and I shall give you something out of Granny's basket for a reward. Another toffee, perhaps – or a pair of knitted gloves – or a piece of Granny's chocolate fudge. You can choose what you would like.'

'I'll unpack the basket for you,' said Daisy, and she lifted off two hot-water bottle covers beautifully knitted by Granny. And then Daisy got such a surprise!

The little white kitten lay curled up in the basket, settled cosily on the knitted gloves! It had crept in there when it felt tired and had fallen fast asleep. It opened big wondering eyes and stood up to stretch itself.

'Oh, Mummy! I brought the kitten home and I didn't know it!' cried Daisy. 'Oh, isn't it sweet?'

The kitten leapt lightly on to the table. It rubbed its soft little head against Mother's hand.

'Mummy, it loves you!' cried Daisy. 'Oh, Mummy, you said I could choose anything out of Granny's basket for a reward – could I, could I have the little white kitten?'

'Miaow,' said the kitten, and rubbed its head against Mother's hand again. She simply couldn't help loving it back.

'Yes, you can have it,' she said. 'It's too sweet for words. I don't like cats, but I've lost my heart to this kitten. I'll ring Granny and tell her we'll keep it if she'll let us!'

'Oh, thank you!' said Daisy. 'No wonder the basket felt heavy. You're mine, kitty. How will you like that?'

'Miaow-*ee-ow-ee-ow*,' said the kitten. And Daisy knew what that meant! 'I shall love being your kitty; you're such a nice little girl!'

Also available:

Enid Blyton
SPRINGTIME STORIES

30 stories

Head off on sparkling
springtime adventures with
these short stories by the
world's best-loved storyteller!